This book belongs to

For my dear friend Pat Bealby

Dorling **DK** Kindersley

LONDON, NEW YORK, SYDNEY, DELHI, PARIS,
MUNICH, and JOHANNESBURG

First published in Great Britain in 1999 by Dorling Kindersley Limited,
9 Henrietta Street, Covent Garden, London WC2E 8PS

This edition published in 2000

2 4 6 8 10 9 7 5 3 1

ISBN 0-7513-6383-9
A CIP catalogue record for this book is available from the British Library.

Colour reproduction by Dot Gradations, UK
Printed and bound in Malaysia by Tien Wah Press

see our complete
catalogue at
www.dk.com

Parsnip

and the **Runaway Tractor**

A Lift-the-Flap Book by **Sue Porter**

DK

A Dorling Kindersley Book

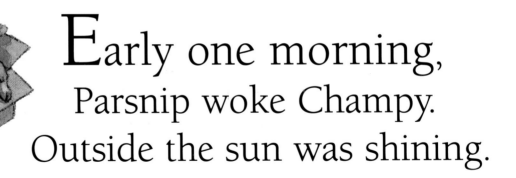

Early one morning,
Parsnip woke Champy.
Outside the sun was shining.

"Wake up, Champy!"

zzzz...

"Look!"

Soon Blanket trotted up, too.
"Climb up!" called Parsnip.

"Now, don't fiddle with the switches," warned Champy's dad.

Champy and Blanket made tractor noises.

"Chug! Chug!"

"Brmm!"

"Brmm!"

"Yum!"

"Yum!"

Tadpole found some sandwiches.

But Parsnip fiddled
with the switches...

The tractor shot forwards

and **crashed** through a haystack.

"Blanket!"

Then it zoomed under

It zig-zagged around the hens and sploshed

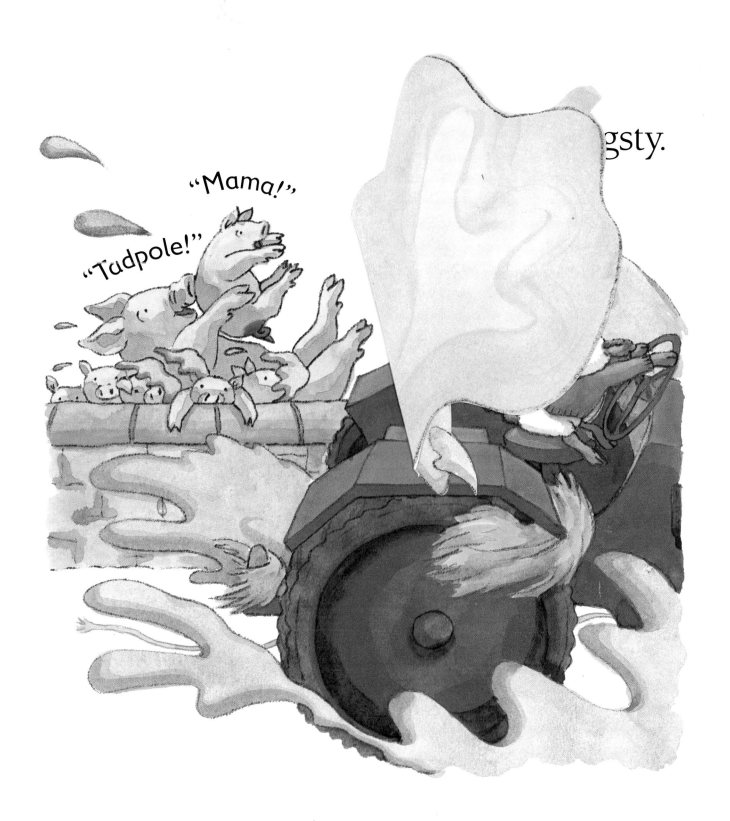

And then the tractor rushed straight towards the duck pond.

"Oh   no!"

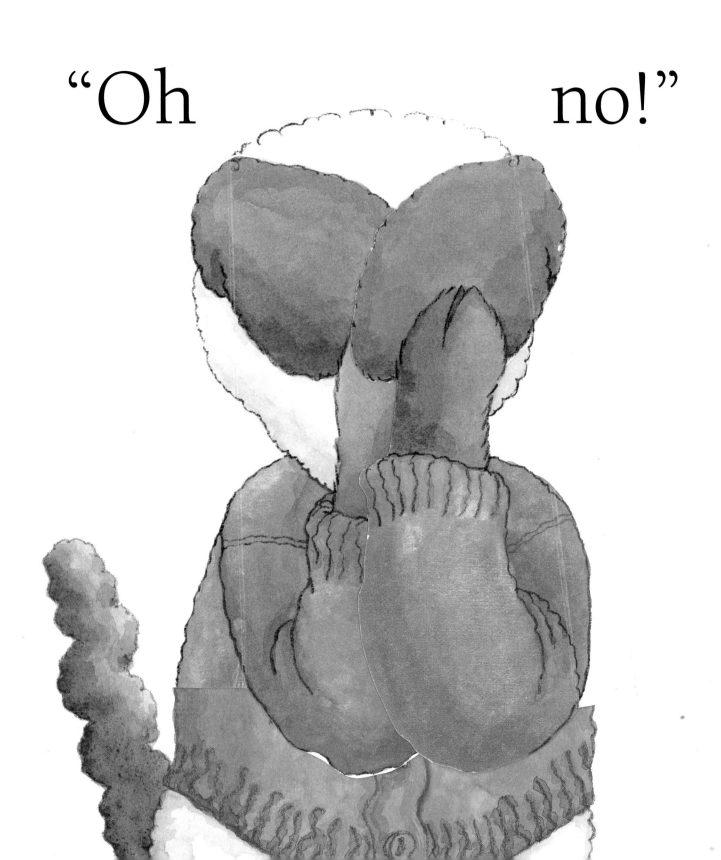

The tractor stopped.

"Mama, help!"

"I promise,
Mama."

Parsnip promised Mama
never to play with tractors again.
Then she cuddled up close.
"Sweet dreams, little Parsnip,"
said Mama.
But Parsnip was already asleep.